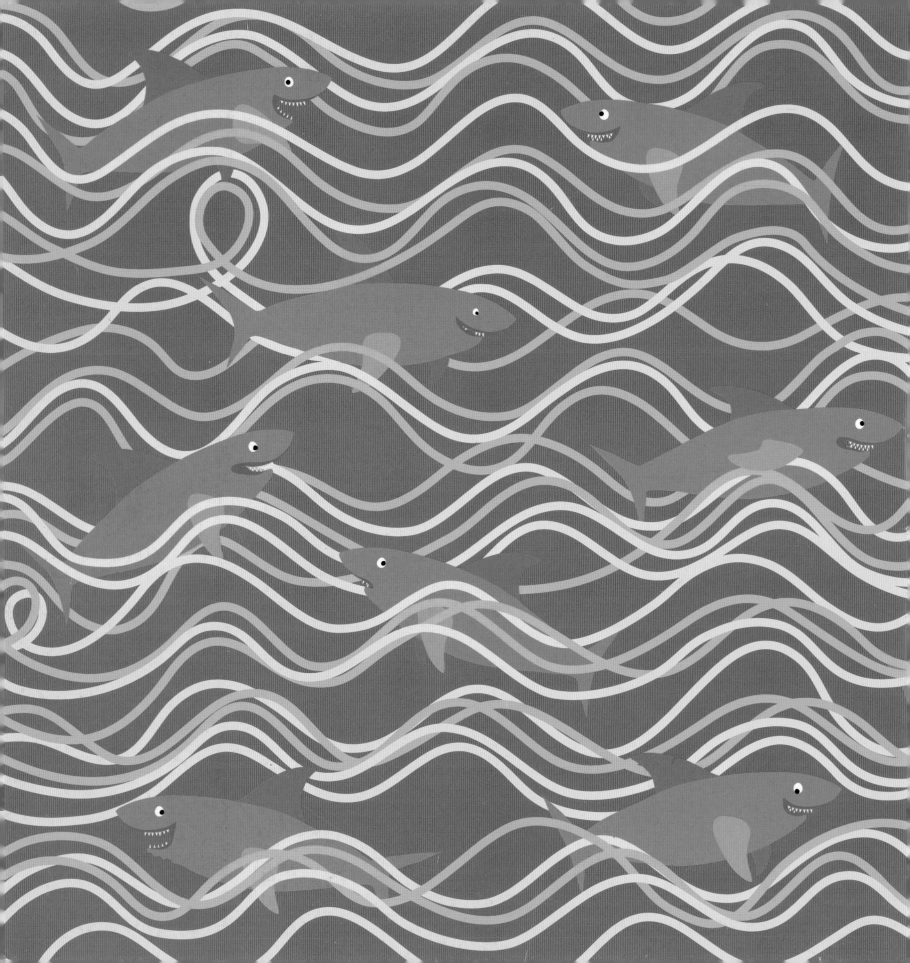

For The Carol Edwards ~ CF

To Macmillan Cancer Support, for all the wonderful work you do ~ SH

Bloomsbury Publishing, London, New Delhi, New York and Sydney
First published in Great Britain in 2015 by Bloomsbury Publishing Plc
50 Bedford Square, London, WC1B 3DP

Text copyright © Claire Freedman 2015
Illustrations copyright © Sue Hendra 2015
The moral rights of the author and illustrator have been asserted

A CIP catalogue record of this book is available from the British Library

ISBN 978 1 4088 5154 8 (HB)
ISBN 978 1 4088 5155 5 (PB)
ISBN 978 1 4088 5153 1 (eBook)

1 3 5 7 9 10 8 6 4 2

Printed in China by Leo Paper Products, Heshan, Guangdong

All papers used by Bloomsbury Publishing are natural, recyclable products made from
wood grown in well-managed forests. The manufacturing processes conform
to the environmental regulations of the country of origin

www.bloomsbury.com

BLOOMSBURY is a registered trademark of Bloomsbury Publishing Plc

MONSTER MAX'S SHARK SPAGHETTI

Claire Freedman

Illustrated by **Sue Hendra**
and **Paul Linnet**

BLOOMSBURY

LONDON NEW DELHI NEW YORK SYDNEY

Max hopes the hotel food tastes yum
but, just in case, he packs
a stash of stale dung beetle crisps —
his favourite smelly snacks!

All monsters fly with Queasy Jet.
Max loves their in-flight meal —

moth mash with tapeworm sausages,
washed down with puréed eel.

Their hotel is delightful,
sticky slug trails paint the walls.
The ceiling's draped with spiders —
wheee! Look out for when one falls!

Fresh caterpillar croissants, SLURP,
are SO good for your health!

CRASH! BANG! comes from the kitchen.
It's the gunkiest you've seen.

The dirty plates are being washed.
One monster licks them clean!

Yippee! It's time to hit the beach.
"It's scorching hot!" Max smiles.

His sunscreen whiffs of rotten eggs,
bugs come from miles and miles!

The beachfront has some super rides.
Max loves the GLOOP-THE-LOOP!
They whizz down chutes of slobber,
splashing through great vats of gloop!

The hotel's pond slime pool is great!
Staff bring scum shakes to sip,
with woodworm riddled loungers,
to relax after your dip!

Max prangs a slimy shark's tooth – PING!
It hits him – YEOWCH! Guess where?

Max has to stand the whole flight home.
His trip won't be forgotten.
He has a special souvenir —
the tooth pulled from his bottom!

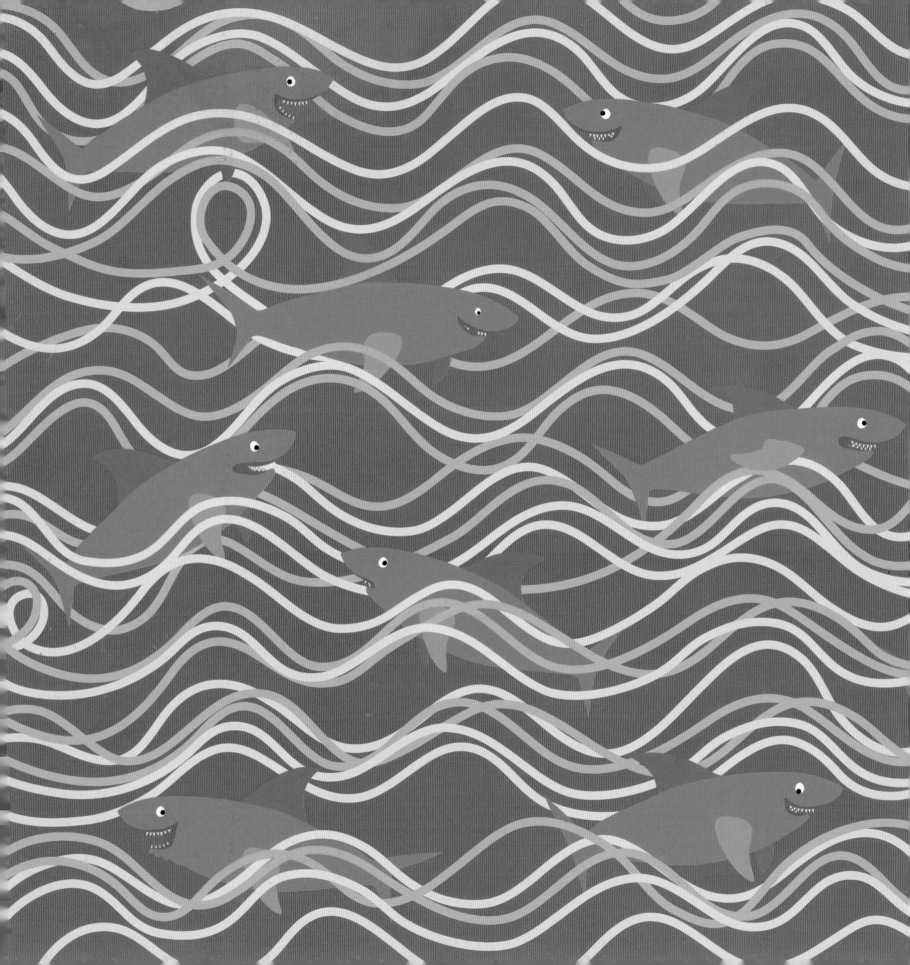

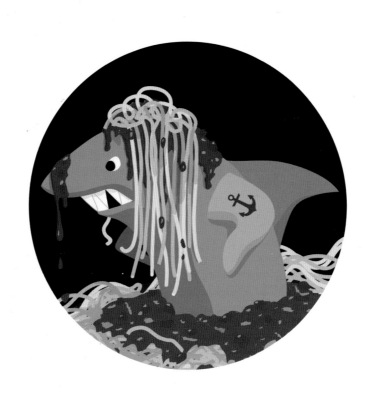